P9-DYE-875

*F*OR PETER AND PETER
B. D.
*F*OR ROSEMARY, MY PARENTS
AND EVERYONE AT WALKER BOOKS
I. A.

Text copyright © 1998 by Berlie Doherty
Illustrations copyright © 1998 by Ian Andrew

All rights reserved.

First U.S. edition 1998

Library of Congress Cataloging-in-Publication Data

Doherty, Berlie.
The midnight man / Berlie Doherty ; illustrated by
Ian Andrew — 1st U.S. ed.
p.   cm.
Summary: One night Harry and his dog follow the
mysterious midnight man on his silent-hooved horse
through the streets and to the edge of the moors before
being returned home by the moon.
ISBN 0-7636-0700-2
[1. Dreams—Fiction.   2. Night—Fiction.]
I. Andrew, Ian P., ill. II. Title.
PZ7.D6947Mi   1998
[E]—dc21   98-3457

2 4 6 8 10 9 7 5 3 1

Printed in Italy

This book was typeset in Tiepolo.
The pictures were done in colored pencil.

Candlewick Press
2067 Massachusetts Avenue
Cambridge, Massachusetts 02140

The Midnight Man

BERLIE DOHERTY

ILLUSTRATED BY IAN ANDREW

CANDLEWICK PRESS

CAMBRIDGE, MASSACHUSETTS

Every night, when Harry and Mister Dog
are asleep, someone comes riding by.

Mister Dog opens one eye and grunts.

Harry opens one eye and yawns.

They both sit up

and gaze out the window,

and this is what they see. . . .

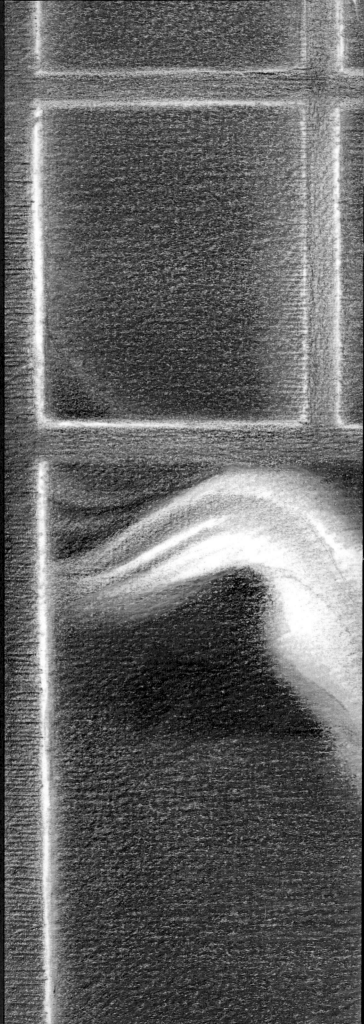

The midnight man comes
riding through the town
on his midnight horse
with its hushing hooves.
His cloak of whispers
swirls around like sighs.
On his hip is a sack of stars.

He pauses, and his horse nods its head and waits.

Then he flings the stars far up to the deep dark sky,

and there they hang and glitter like flowers of ice.

And some come sprinkling over Mister Dog,

around his nose, and make him sneeze.

And some brush against Harry's face and dust his eyes.

"Who is it?" whispers Harry.

"Woof!" woofs Mister Dog.

They tiptoe downstairs, past all the snoring doors,

and they're out and up the street

before the latch clicks shut.

The midnight man goes riding on his midnight horse,

and all the black shadow cats slink around

his midnight-quiet hooves.

"Wait for me!" Harry shouts, but his voice is soft as mist,

and his feet make sounds like hushes on the ground.

"Woof!" woofs Mister Dog,

but his woof has turned to shush,

and his paws are faint as feathers

as he trots along behind.

"You can't come with me!" The midnight man laughs.

His voice is like owl cries and fox calls far away.

"I have the world to travel.

There's no resting place for me."

But still they call, and still they run,
and still they make no sound . . .
down the streets and over bridges,
under arches, through the trees,

till they come to the last house
at the very end of town,
where the moors stretch into darkness
as if there's no world left.

And softer and fainter go the pittering midnight hooves.

"No resting place for me. My home is midnight land."

The midnight man turns once . . .

and once he waves his hand.

Harry and Mister Dog lie sleeping on the ground

where the moors stretch away to the end of the world.

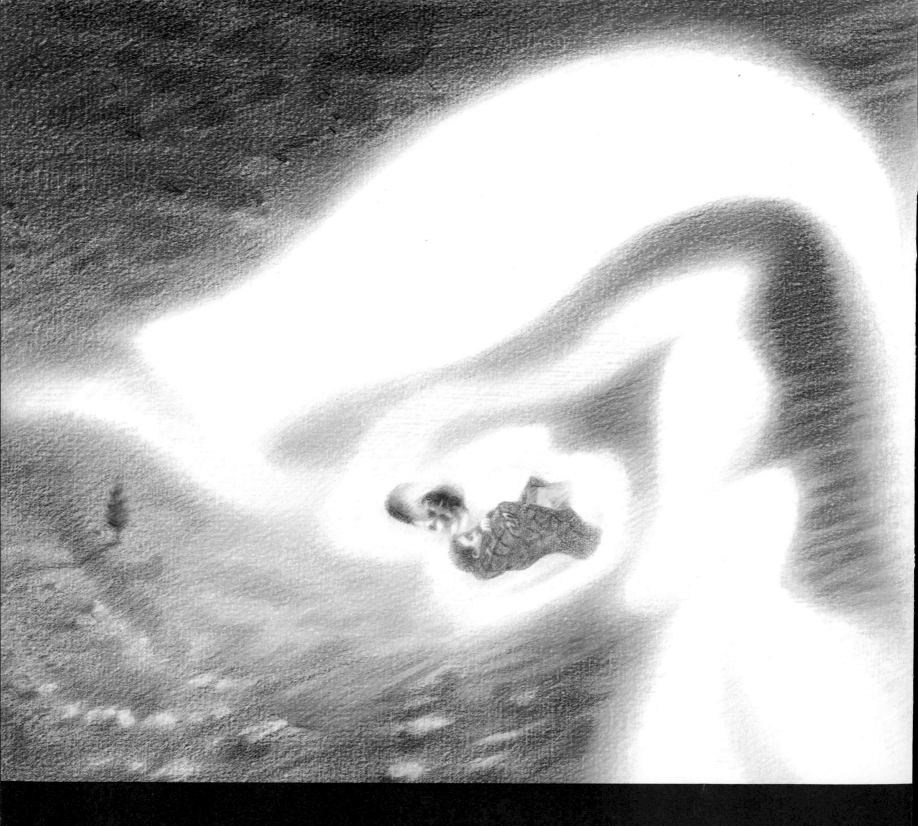

But the white moon sees as she swings across the sky.

She slides down the darkness and peers at them and cries.

She cradles them into her creamy arms and sways back

through the trees where the midnight man had been . . .

under arches, over bridges, down the streets,

past the slinking shadow cats

to the door of Harry's house,

with the latch clicked shut.

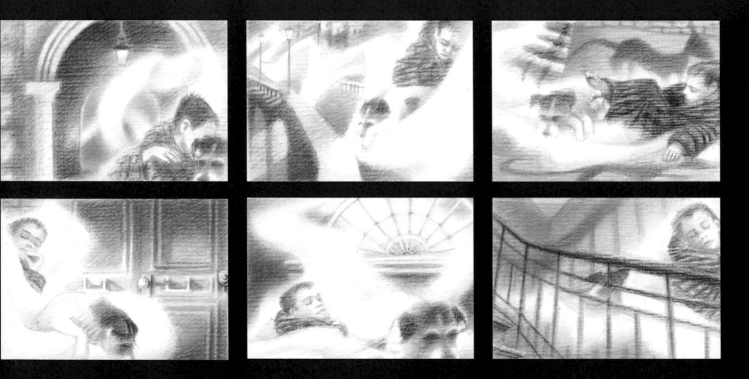

She streams through the window

and glides up the tiptoe stairs

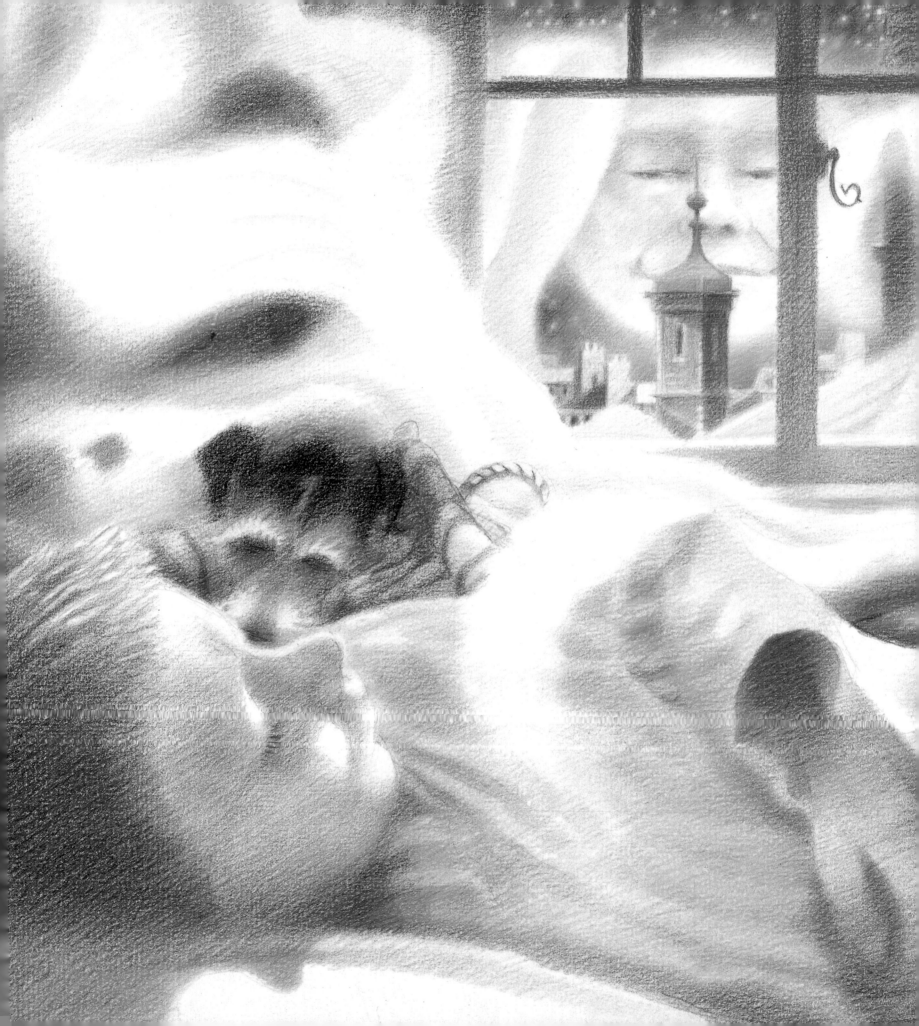

slipping through the starry sky.

They seem to hear a midnight horse

galloping on midnight hooves.

And do they hear a midnight voice,

laughing like owl cries and fox calls,

"Woof!" woofs Mister Dog.

They brush the stardust from their eyes

and sleep till morning comes.